mouth

SHO

EYMOUTH

TEDDY BEARS WOULD GO TO TEDDY BEAR WOODS
TEDDY BEARS WOULD GO TO TEDDY BEAR WOODS

The Bank of Dreams & Nightmares
20 Rax Lane, Bridport, DT6 3JJ

www.thebankofdreamsandnightmares.org

Published June 2023

Workshop leader
Rowan Beecham

Volunteer story mentors
Raja Jarrah
Georgina Bowman
Vix Brown
Eleanor James
Rosie Russell
Imi Neylan

Partner teacher
Mark Cavill

Designer
Spike Golding

Map illustrator
Helen Cann

Photography
Eddy Pearce

ISBN: 978-1-7397340-4-6
Printed in Exeter by Imprint books

Don't feed the locals!

GUIDE TO WEYMOUTH BY YOUNG WRITERS FROM BUDMOUTH ACADEMY

GUIDE TO WEYMOUTH BY YOUNG WRITERS FROM BUDMOUTH ACADEMY

Don't feed the locals!

FOREWORD

by Joanna Quinn

One of the most magical things about creative writing is that it can make the ordinary extraordinary. It can turn the everyday upside down and transform it into something beautiful, funny, scary, weird or wonderful. The talented young writers in this anthology have done just that. They have looked at their home town of Weymouth and they have re-imagined it.

Familiarity breeds contempt and it's very easy to let the things we see in our daily lives become flat and two-dimensional. We assume there is nothing interesting about our local shops or our local area, because we have seen them so many times before.

But there are always new ways to see things and, as this book shows, writing about a place allows us to look at it with fresh eyes. We can describe it in ways it has never been described before. We can imagine what it used to be in the past and what it might be in the future. What a gift that is!

In this guidebook you will find top tips on how to spend your time in Weymouth – a town of 'heavenly smells' where the sun shines down like a 'gigantic heat lamp' and where adults become enraged by arcade games. There's plenty to do, whether you want to swim with mermaids, find a secret passage where fairies roam or join the chanting fans at Weymouth FC. You can also read short stories inspired by the town, that feature everything from a demonic baker to a theatrical ghost – and there's an interview with one of the town's best-known residents.

Too often creativity is seen as something that only some people have, but imagination is something everyone has. And what better way to use it than to join these students in celebrating our own special part of the world.

PLAY LIST

WEYMOUTH

NEWTON'S

Contents

Cardigan by Taylor S
Jack Johnson, The Cl
Blowin' in the wind b
Coldplay, The kids do
Declan McKenna, Ocea
Man by Conan Gray, M
by Nina Simone, Cinn
Ray, Darkside by Neo
West, Coast by Lana D
by Pixies, Golden Ho
Bruno Mars, Going to t
Brazil by Declan Mcl
Don't worry be h
Wildest Dreams by Ta

vift, Upside Down by
in by Fleetwood Mac
Bob Dylan, Yellow by
wanna come home by
Man by Ween, Family
baby just cares for me
mon Girl by Lana Del
Glimpse of us by Joji
Ray, Where's my mind
by Juke, Treasure by
Bank by Commodores
nna, Believe by Cher
py Bobby McFerrin
or Swift

Introduction

Weymouth is a wonderful seaside town in Dorset with many hidden gems ready to be explored. In our guidebook you will find treasures unseen in any other guidebook; we will show you things that you would never have imagined you would find by yourself and walk you through the rich history of our little town. Weymouth is so much more than just a summer tourist attraction, but if it is summer and you are a tourist, this guidebook is for you too!

What's so important about Weymouth, why is it the place to be? Dip your toes in the refreshing comfort of the Weymouth sea. Enjoy the busy murmur of the thriving town as people rush into coffee shops. Weymouth isn't just a place, it's a home.

This guidebook was brought to you by the creative students aged 14 and 15 years old from Budmouth Academy and The Bank of Dreams & Nightmares.

Students' thoughts:

"When I was picked for helping write the book I was excited to be an actual author writing about Weymouth. When I met the staff at The Bank Of Dreams and Nightmares, they were extremely friendly and comfortable to be around. Since then, we have written ghost stories, interviewed pigeons, written poems, drawn maps and explored Weymouth. Helping write this book has been an experience I will never forget."

"When I was picked for writing the book I thought that we would just be working on a book. However that could not be more untrue; we have done so many more fun things alongside working on the book."

"I was excited when I found out that we'd be writing a book that would be published. In the first workshop we met the staff and they were very welcoming and friendly. My favourite session we did was either the map drawing or the story writing but I have enjoyed all the sessions. I will always remember the fun I had while writing this book and it has been a fantastic experience. Thank you."

"When we started this project I wasn't really sure about what we were going to be doing, but now I have loved coming to the workshops every week, and have been made to feel very comfortable sharing my ideas and I have absolutely loved this whole experience."

There is nothing better about Weymouth than...

The dinosaurs running around the Jurassic coast. They are running around like champion runners! They always loved their McDonalds, every now and then, but they normally have spaghetti. They are not all about McDonalds and spaghetti because they invented the Iron Man event to keep fit (not healthy). The first winner of the Iron Man event was Johnny Rex, Johnny came first using his amazing skills... in basically everything! TYLER

Walking my dog through the luscious lime fields, wind breezing through the soft, tall grass packed with dandelions. Sky blue, waves crashing and turning pearl white. The scent of salty fish and chips... DOMINIK

The atmosphere when I am with my friends hanging out at the arcade, or walking and shopping around town. Going to the Pavilion with my family, having a good laugh when there's a joke or the cast make a mistake. Going on the beach, playing in the sea with friends; the feeling of the fresh salty sea when I get in, the coldness makes me feel like my body is awoken again. DALIA

The arcade at Alexander gardens - riding the cars there makes me feel happy when I'm with my sisters. The beach, the boats, the rides, it makes me feel happy when I am with my family. CHLOE

Strolling across the beach of an evening, hearing the wail of the seagulls, desperate for any food they can get. The smell of chips filling my nose as I walk past. One time, when I was young I had just finished a big whippy ice cream and I had a pretend ice cream in my other hand, a seagull came and took the pretend one! Another best place is the bubble tea shop, especially one called Drinc Inc. and I love the fish and chips from Marlboro. FREYA

Walking through town on a rainy day, the droplets pitter pattering around me. Seeing the nearly empty streets, I can hear the subtle tapping of my shoes on the cobbled roads. Suddenly the pitter pattering becomes crashing and clattering, pouring and pelting and almost as fast as the rain quickens, I do too!

As I'm running through the town on this very rainy day, seeming to be looking for some kind of shelter, I am laughing as I secretly wish that this rainy day will never end. LILY

The magic of the atmosphere inside the Pavillion while watching the panto and enjoying the magic of Christmas.

The feeling of Christmas in town when there's the ice rink and Christmas lights, a feeling of satisfaction.

Ice cream parlours, all along the beach, it's a great attraction and a great place to stop when it's hot outside.

The feeling of when it is cold outside and you go into Caffé Nero. You get a lovely hot drink and it fills you with so much excitement and joy. You're wrapped up cosy in scarves and lots of layers. You take a sip of your drink and the cream leaves a line above your lip.

The water is so clear and crystaline almost hypnotising you. If there's a full moon and you touch the water, then you turn into a mermaid.

In the Nothe Fort, if you are lucky, you can fire a cannon just like back in the day!

Weymouth library, there is entertainment for everyone, including a sensory setting for children and books of all genres to let your imagination run free! JAIMEY

The fish and chip shops because it is fresh. The beach is also nice because it has really clear water, perfect for swimming or even rock pooling (fishing for crabs, shrimp and fish). Another thing I like about the fish and chip shop is that the fish are caught in Weymouth, which makes all the fish they sell so fresh and tasty. Daniel's fish and chip shop is my favourite, because it usually has mackerel which is my favourite fish to eat and all the people are so nice inside the shop, they don't rush you when you don't know what to get, or in any other situation. When we got my fish and chips I would usually go to the beach to eat, but sometimes I will just go home. KAYDEN

The arcades, there are so many good games to play and prizes to win.

The fish and chip shops, the fish are caught here in Weymouth, so it's fresh. Going to the Pavilion with friends, there are so many amazing shows to watch which are worth the little money you pay.

Running across the beach at night is fun and peaceful, feeling the sand against your feet as the moonlight is the only thing lighting up the beach. BLAIR

Rossi's ice cream (especially vanilla flavour).
The amusements, losing all your money to a 2p machine.
Getting bubble teas and going shopping.
Dipping your feet into the ocean.
The smell of the sea.
The pebbles that hurt your feet if you walk too far on the beach.
The little trains that tour around Weymouth.
The huge fish at Fish and Fritz.
The Sea Life Centre.
Going to the beach when it's raining.
Fish and Chips.
Food being stolen by vicious seagulls.
Going to the harbour and getting ice cream.
Seeing buckets of crabs everywhere and people catching them.
Bars and ice cream places along the harbour.
Marlborough fish cakes.
Rainbow coloured houses near Asda.
Playing basketball or air hockey in the amusements.
EVIE

Sea Life/ Sea Life train (if with young children)
Rossi's ice cream
Weymouth library
Nothe Fort
Sandsfoot/Sandsfoot gardens
Swannery Walk (feeding ducks and swans)
Dog walk places
Seafood festival
Walking on the beach (in winter)
Café Monet
MAISIE

Arcade
The Marsh
Suttons café
Sandworld
Sea Life land train
Lodmore, green gym,
Sandsfoot gardens
Rodwell trail
Radipole lane- Black death
Weymouth Pavilion
Rossi's ice cream
Marlboro fish and chips shop
Bowleaze cove
Bowleaze fun park, beach, hire paddleboards in the summer
Nothe fort, find the mice (one is hidden in the painting)
Newton's cove
The Fleet
Iron man, beach motocross
Fireworks and bonfire night
CHRISTABELLE

Visiting the beach with friends and going swimming , getting some food and going to the arcade, getting photos taken in the photo booth.

Top 10 things to do
The beach
The Pavilion
The Fleet, walking to Portland
Sandsfoot gardens, hidden gem viewpoint
Radipole nature reserve to feed the swans
Sea Life Centre, interactive activities
Lodmoor park, peaceful golf trail, outdoor gym park, RSPB and playpark
Nothe fort, gardens walking, nature squirrels, history
Alexandra gardens food, sitting, eating, kiosks, games
The seafront and the esplanade, the walks and the views
MIA

Fieldtrip

What a wonderful journey we experienced. We witnessed big and small discoveries all with their own unique stories.

Walking along we met the sea swimmers, who dare to go in the sea in any kind of weather. At Nothe Fort we went through a deep thicket with twisting turning trees, everything there had a tale. How ancient it grows as we relax under the warm refreshing breeze. Moving along we strode to the harbour below, the boats swinging left to right. Whenever a new boat arrives it pushes the water away. Slowly pacing down we saw all the colourful boats, we glanced at this longboat being freshly painted. Shy at first we got the guts to talk and ask questions to the painters, a boat race they answered, they were painting the boat a bright crimson red for the boat to look fabulous for the next race. We did not stop and strode along to reach the lifting bridge blooming with red and green colours, opening up every two hours. Crossing over it we reached the town where all the shops are. We were feeling tempted to go to Mcdonalds but we couldn't stop!! As we continued we found ourselves outside a bubble tea shop with blissful flavours that our taste buds died for. We all got different bubble teas that brought us delight. As we adventured on we came to the beach, looking across at the smooth pastel yellow sand merging together with the crystal sea. We walked down the esplanade and had a small break for lunch.

After we energised ourselves we continued our journey to reach the hidden library; a library with all the books you could think of. We sat down noting what we have discovered. Exhausted with smiles on our faces we headed back to school, away from our adventure.

'S COVE

Weymouth

Reviews

WEYMOUTH

THE
DREAM
SHOP

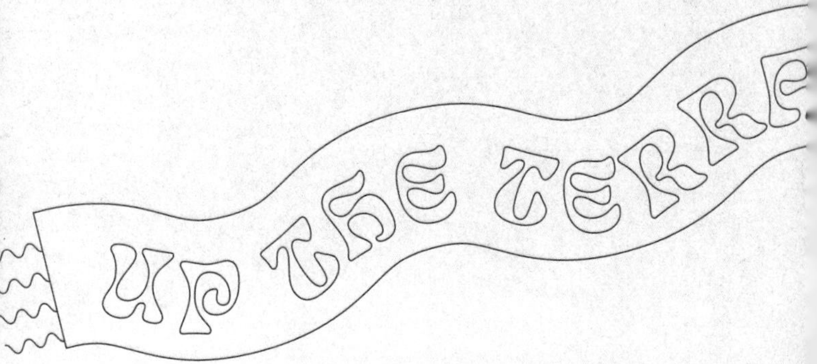
UP THE TERR

TEDDY BEARS
TO TEDDY BEAR WOODS GO
TEDDY BEARS WOULD GO TO TEDDY BEAR WOODS

1

Weymouth FC

www.uptheterras.co.uk

"Come on the Terras!"

Bob Lucas Stadium. It all starts after parking along Radipole Lane as the main car park will be too crammed to even get in or out. You will literally get stuck. No matter what. Full of anticipation, take a walk up the road and cross just at the top near the roundabout. Head into the entrance and go up through the cars belonging to people who have made the regrettable decision to park there. Follow the road and you will instantly smell the sense of salty chips. Be sure to get to the match around half an hour before kick-off to avoid queues at the turnstiles; either have your ticket on your phone or a season ticket, or you can buy on the day although that's not as reliable. Right at the top on the right you will find the best entrance with two signs above indicating which one to go in. Walk through,allow your ticket to be scanned by the friendly guy on the left and then push through the metal rods and be released into the land of relief.

Soon you will be buzzing from excitement, take it all in, and head round to behind the goal. That is where the loudest chants will constantly take place. Now to be indulged in the game, although don't bank on a win if it's a Saturday watching the men though. If it's chips you desire, do buy them just before half time as if not it has to be admitted that they aren't always as crispy as you may like if you leave it till the rush.

After the game it is best to go out the exit towards the left of the goal on the top of the steps as that allows you to be free down the road. And enjoy it - I'm sure you will be captured!

Bob Lucas Stadium,
Radipole Lane, DT4 9XJ
///dangerously.charge.
assure

2

Curtis Fields

A magical place to go for a walk or a stroll especially in the spring when the flowers are sprouting and the air is crisp turning warm. Relax and enjoy your surroundings as you watch the sunset like someone once asked me to do on a date. If you go here you will gain so much rizz.

It's peaceful and comforting and a beautiful place to take your dog on a walk or for a first date. There is a secret passage where fairies roam and thrive, if you're quiet enough they might come out and say hello. I remember when I took my friend for her first time and we ended up getting lost but it's okay because it was easy to find our way again, following the gorgeous blossoms that led me to where I needed to be.

If you want to impress a girl, this is the place to go. Even just to sit and talk, it's such a romantic venue especially at sunset and sunrise.

/// asks.dinner.cave

"Relax and enjoy your surroundings."

3

The Dream Shop

Open all week / aldi.co.uk/weymouth

"The staff at both of the ALDIs are extremely friendly and will help you with anything you need."

You may think ALDI is just a shop but to me it's more. ALDI is the most special store as it has almost everything I need like special buys, toys, health and beauty, wine and spirits and groceries. The special buys are so amazing I once snuck out of my house just to go see the new ones they had put up and got grounded. ALDI's special buys consist of everything from toys, beauty and health, house decor and exclusive food that won't be sold there again. There are two ALDIs in Weymouth, one at 457 Chickerell Road and one located at Mercury Road. The staff at both of the ALDIs are extremely friendly and will help you with anything you need. My favourite ALDI is the one on Chickerell Road as I have many memories connected to there and I know all of the workers on a friend level as I am there so often. One of my favourite memories is when I got my shopping free because my mother had lost her card and the man behind me paid for our shopping. When I walk into ALDI I get hit with a warm breeze.

I always know where the special buys are as there are massive signs hanging from the ceiling, the bright blue as the background making the white writing spelling "Special Buys" stand out. Both of the ALDIs have other shops surrounding them, the one on Mercury Road has a New Look, Sainsburys, Mcdonalds and a petrol station. The other ALDI has a Starbucks, Burger King, Greggs and behind the ALDI there's a Screwfix and a vet along with a bunch of other shops I cannot remember off the top of my head.

Link Park, Chickerell
Link Road, DT3 4FL
///input.term.exit

5

McDonalds

Open all week / McDonalds.com

Did you know that the McDonald's M is the Weymouth W upside down?

When I go into McDonalds I can smell burgers, fries, chicken nuggets and maybe some drinks. It looks like a house but it's not. Inside McDonalds at the door there is an "order yourself something to eat" then you can go to the cashier and pay for the food then you wait until they say your number. The number is like 098. Inside the McDonald's there are a lot of tables and chairs and there are toilets. I get chicken nuggets and fries with a medium Coca-Cola.

There are three McDonalds - one in town, one near town and there is one behind Morrisons. The first one is St Mary Street and the second one is Jubilee Close retail park and the third one is 2 Souter Way.

When you're waiting for your order number to be called you can go on your phone or stand there if you want.

You can get this new burger called McCrispy.

What I like about this is the crispy chicken because it's spicy and it's nice to chew but your mouth will get a bit hot and the bun is soft and it has a lot of seeds all over the bun and I think the mayo is garlic mayo.

Retail Park Jubilee Close
Jubilee Close, DT4 7BG
///humans.remit.extra

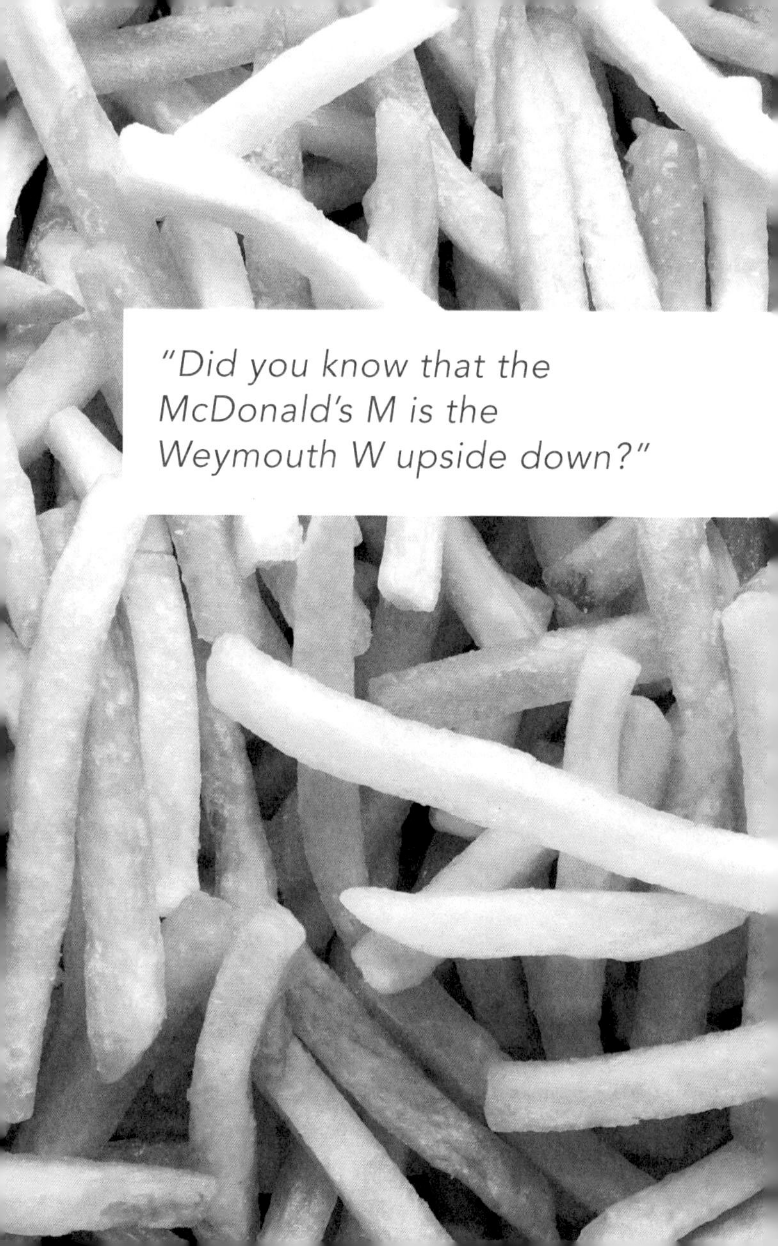

"Did you know that the McDonald's M is the Weymouth W upside down?"

6

The Library

dorsetcouncil.gov.uk/w/weymouth-lending-library

"Relaxing, quiet and comfy."

From the moment that I entered this library, I was met with an extremely calm and peaceful atmosphere. Weymouth Library, although hidden away on a backstreet of the town centre, has been described by customers as 'relaxing', 'quiet' and 'comfy'.

The library hosts a variety of fun and interactive events, including art workshops, coding and lego clubs, toddler and baby groups ('rhymetime') meeting reptiles and many more. In addition to this, the library has many computers for public use, books with extremely varied genres and age ranges, and a kid's area with many sensory and colourful activities.

Although it comes with many pros, all establishments have their flaws. Obviously it is a library, so the books have been taken home and read by many people before reaching your hands. Many of the books have folded or slightly damaged pages. The library does replace the books if they are in too bad of a condition, however if you are looking for a book in perfect condition, the library is probably not the best choice.

Another minor problem is the all ages aspect. The library is quiet for the majority of the time, but often there are small, excitable children that also find reading enjoyable. Most children - in my experience of the library - respect the values of the library and stay extremely quiet. Occasionally there is a toddler or small child, however, who will be a little chatty or loud. This is usually nothing to worry about but if your goal is to read in silence, this could be slightly distracting.

Overall though, the library is an incredible place to spend a quiet afternoon, especially on a rainy day. The majority of the people that I have spoken to have highlighted the incredibly comfy chairs that are dotted around the library and kid's area. They have been described mostly as 'comfy and colourful' and are adored by local children. I would definitely recommend Weymouth Library, it is a place for everyone.

Great George St,
Melcombe Regis, DT4 8NN
/// medium.ripe.flip

7

Electric Palace

Open all week

"The delayed scoop of the ticket scooper."

There's nothing better about Weymouth than the arcade. I absolutely love the arcade the lights, tickets, the sound of a whiny child after I beat him in Mario Kart, the skill required to get a jackpot at the Paw Patrol spinner, the sound of the same whiny kid after I beat him at the hungry hungry hippos, the delayed scoop of the ticket scooper, the flapping of the birds in flying tickets, the maniacal laughter of a child who bought his backpack in the ball drop, the angry stomping of the whiny kid whose highscore I beat at bowling, the rageful shouting of an adult who can't beat the claw game, the flow of tickets entering a counter and the sense of accomplishment that you get when you get that prize you've been saving up for!

The Esplanade
Melcombe Regis, DT4 8DL
/// yours.tube.repay

Flying
5 Plays for £1
20p
PRIZE OUT

10

Teddy Bear Woods

I went for a walk there and it was beautiful.

Although it was quite small for a forest it was a tremendous sight with wildlife quite abundant despite it mostly being cut down. It's also a very quiet place despite it being quite near a usually very noisy park. Overall an absolutely lovely time just don't eat any orange or red berries and stick to the blackberries just outside the woods they taste and smell lovely.

Castlemaine Road
DT3 6HU
///rotations.acclaimed.towns

"I went for a walk there and it was beautiful."

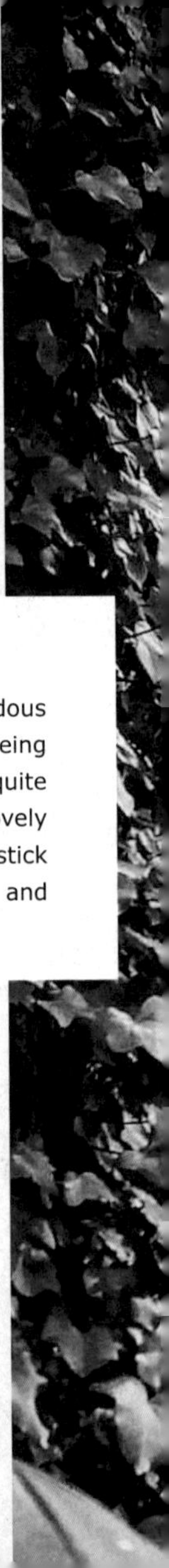

11

Oasis Cafe

Mon- Sat, 8-4.30 / Cafeoasis.co.uk

"Leave your stress at home!"

As I approached the Oasis Cafe I noticed the beautiful blue mural complementing the sapphire ocean next door. The peaceful ambient sound of waves crashing satisfied my ears.

I sat down on the cushioned open-air chairs and ordered my meal: King Prawns with Garlic and Chilli. It was amazing: the side salad had fresh, juicy produce; the bread was the perfect amount of crispness; and finally the prawns. Oh the prawns... If only I could eat them all day. It was bliss. It felt as if I was in heaven. It was scrumptious.

The staff were very funny, interactive and gave me fabulous advice on what to order on the playful and varied menu. Everything was different from one another; from homemade cheeseburgers to lemon and oregano chicken skewers.

The sweet, pastel coloured walls comforted me with vintage wine bottles filling the soft ambience. The pictures, that were next to the windows, continued the landscape of the foamy sea and golden pebbles.

You can park in the expensive car park next to the cafe or you could take the luscious stroll across the esplanade, seeing families enjoying the sun like a gigantic heat lamp shining down upon them and the wind surfers catching waves like picking flowers from a lime field or the cyclists riding next to you like they are on a journey across the world. Eventually you'll reach your destination - the Oasis Cafe.

Overcombe Corner,
Bowleaze Coveway,
DT3 6PN
///sweat.tunnel.heartened

13

Lodmoor Park

Park open all week

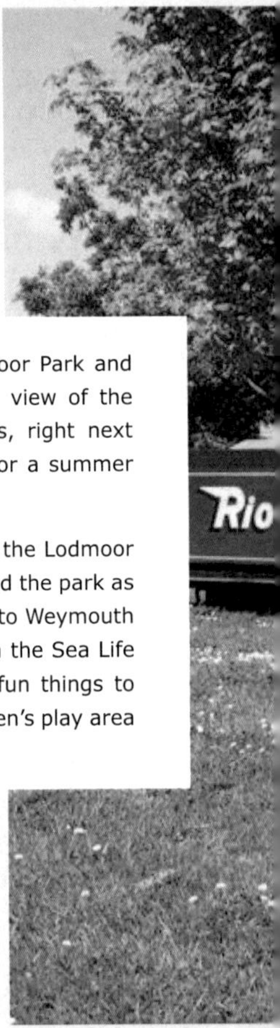

The Lodmoor train goes all around Lodmoor Park and gives you a relaxing ride and a detailed view of the park. A hidden gem found in the woods, right next to a Kelly's ice cream shop and perfect for a summer adventure.

Children and adults love going around on the Lodmoor train and it's perfect for a quick tour around the park as it is only 10 minutes long. It is very close to Weymouth beach and is only a short walk away from the Sea Life Centre. Lodmoor Park also has a lot of fun things to do like gym equipment, Go-Karting, children's play area and a restaurant close by.

Greenhill Road,
DT4 7SX
/// fortunate.drifters.brilliant

"A perfect summer adventure."

14

The Sea Life Centre

Open all week /sealifeweymouth.com

The Sea Life Centre is located by the beach, a golf course and a place to go and eat food.

A story I was told was when this person was 6 years old their mum loved penguins so when they went into the Sea Life Centre they went to the penguin exhibit and tried to get inside. Luckily someone stopped them but it was a funny story anyway.

I recommend this for kids mainly because I remember when I was little I found the different marine life very interesting. Some parents also are interested but mainly only kids are interested.

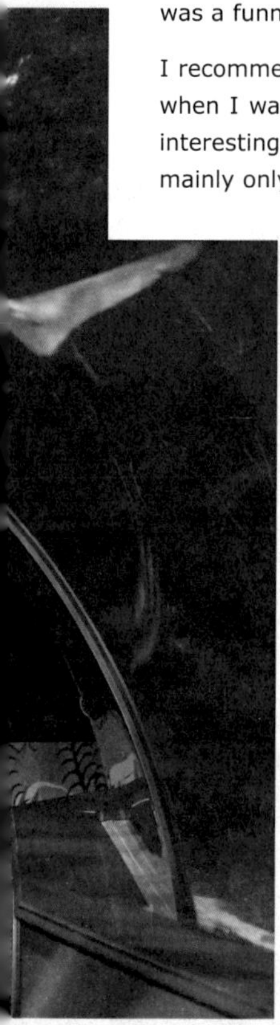

Lodmoor Country Park
Preston Beach Road
DT4 7SX
/// panics.dignitary.reveal

"Some parents also are interested but mainly only kids are interested."

15

The Oxygen Ride at Alexander Gardens

Oxygen Ride is currently not here but we love it anyway. Alexander Gardens is open all week

The arcade is a place that I would choose to go for my days off just because of how fun it is. The tickets for rides are little coins that are usually £1 and most of the time it is only £1 per ride but there are some that are more than £1 per ride.

There is a wide variety of things you can get with tickets. Most things are expensive but that means there is more time to have fun and earn more tickets.

My favourite part of the arcade is the pirate spin wheel because I've won up to 5000 tickets on it but it does take some luck. My friend's favourite part is the one where you have a toy hammer and have to hit it at a certain strength to hit the top which is 1000 tickets. Alexandra Gardens has been around since 1910, meaning even more than 100 years ago people were still having a very good time. Alexandra Gardens is right next to the beach and close to fish and chips shops, McDonalds and more eating places.

I have many good memories connected to the arcade at Alexandra Gardens, especially the VR headset game.

A main memory is when I told my friend I was putting an adventure game on the VR but put a horror one on instead and I could hear them screaming through the sounds of the game. The VR is £3 for two people and £2 for one and has a massive variety of different games including interactive ones.

The Oxygen is a ride just left of Alexandra Gardens and is 130 metres in the air and you also go upside down. There is a height limit of 5ft so you don't fall off the ride. It's £3 per person and is a ride I would definitely recommend.

Overcombe Corner,
Bowleaze Coveway,
Weymouth DT3 6PN
/// lights.slurred.obliging

16

Howley's Toymaster

Open all week / howleys.co.uk

Are you a fan of TOYS?
Are your kids fans of TOYS?
Do you want dolls, FUNKO Pops, Lego or anything else?
If so, Howley's TOYMASTER is the place for you!

They offer many different kinds of FUNKO Pops, ranging from pop culture, royalty, video games and music. As well as more obscure things like Airfix models and a large display of model animals.

The feeling you get when you walk up the ramp into the shop, a wave of nostalgia flows over you and the bright welcoming atmosphere immediately draws you in. The smell and the sounds are warm, child-like and incredibly inviting.

The beach merchandise available can prepare you for a day of fun on Weymouth beach, which is just opposite! There is everything from buckets and spades and beach balls to bodyboards and crabbing kits! Quality items for a fair price!

- D and D
- Candyplanet
- Dolls
- Plushies
- Lego
- Lots of sales
- Nice staff, understanding

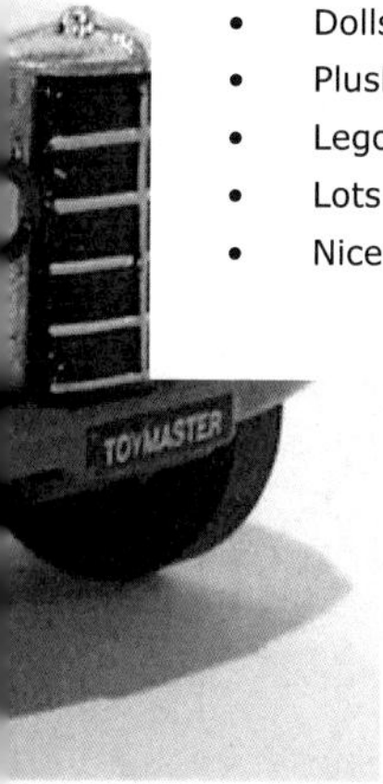

4-5 Frederick Place
DT4 8HQ
/// slime.gains.ripe

17

Ming Wah

Tue- Sun, 4.45-10.30 / mingwah.co.uk

Here in Weymouth you'll find many different restaurants and takeaways all with delicious food. But all unlike this amazing place: Ming Wah located at St. Thomas Street. This unique restaurant and takeaway has all the mouth watering food that a Chinese restaurant could imagine.

As soon as you walk in you get hit by the mesmerising smell of all the food lingering in the air. The atmosphere gives you that welcoming feeling from all the staff. The noises you hear give you that sense of life to it, such as the chattering from the hungry families, the clattering of all the dishes in the restaurant and in the kitchen, and the soothing traditional melody playing in the background. Outside you'll see the growing plant watching you silently as you enter in. Inside you'll see the multiple crimson tables all neatly prepared for your arrival. And the gliding bloomed-coloured fish swimming in their tank watching over everyone's feast.

You must come and try because there is always enough or even too much to devour, a wide variety of food for everyone, like the Spicy Singapore rice noodles, appetizing House special fried rice with sauce or even the Delicious Duck with pancakes and sauce. They are open Tuesday till Sunday (5pm-10pm) waiting for you whenever you are desperate for a flavoursome Chinese meal.

So come on down, this is the absolute must to go and eat in Weymouth!

86 St. Thomas Street, DT4 8EN
///leaps.decent.type

"The absolute must go and eat in Weymouth."

18

Roly's Fudge

Open all week / Rolysfudge.co.uk

"A hidden gem in Weymouth!"

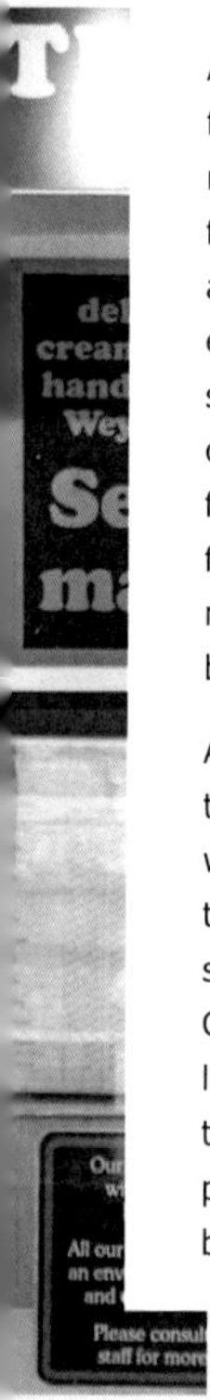

As soon as you walk into the shop your nose is blessed with a variety of heavenly smells. Over 15 different flavours of mouthwatering fudge ranging from traditional flavours such as vanilla clotted cream, chocolate and maple and walnut, as well as some more contemporary flavours such as salted maple and pecan. My personal favourite flavour is cherry bakewell because it tastes exactly like it says and it melts in your mouth as soon as it lands on your tongue. They also have seasonal flavours during Hallowe'en and Christmas.

Another fantastic feature is that they offer vegan and dairy free fudge: salted maple and pecan, when available. The fudge is made fresh everyday by hand using local ingredients from local farmers using a traditional copper pan. A selection of flavours are made everyday so you can't have the flavour you want everytime but there are plenty more to choose from. You can select how much fudge you want so you can have a few pieces or lots of fudge or you can select one of the pre-made bags of fudge which has lots of unique flavours. The 5 original flavours from the first Roly's Fudge shop in 1987 (vanilla, chocolate, maple and walnut, butterscotch and rum 'n' raisin) can still be bought today.

As you walk past the shop, you can watch in the window the fudge bubbling in the copper pan and being stirred by a wooden spoon in the hands of super friendly staff. You can find the shop off the high street, a few doors up from the Drinc Inc shop. There are over 45 Roly's Fudge shops across the UK from Cornwall all the way up north to the Lake District and we're lucky enough to have one here in Weymouth. When you visit the different locations across the UK, you can look forward to purchasing the fudge from the different Roly's Fudge shops because you know how fantastic and what good value it will be.

20 St Alban Street
DT4 8BZ
///twist.yours.allows

19

The Fair

When I last went to the fair I was so excited for the fun that lay ahead.

There's infinite fun since everytime you go it's got brand new rides!

The fastest of the rides are the best since they give you a certain feeling, like an explosion of enjoyment inside, conquering your fears.

The fair is open for all ages including rides for the younger kids.They can go onto the ferris wheel for an amazing experience.

It's located near the Pavilion on the seafront, and since it's on the seafront you can get fish and chips wherever you look (may be quite expensive). McDonalds may be a cheaper alternative in town that's not that far away.

If you want to go to the fair you should take around £20 to get the full enjoyment from all the rides; being able to go on ones you loved again.

Sometimes the people working seem a little grumpy since they always watch other people having so much fun.

But remember it's only open at certain times, mainly on school holidays so they can bring more people enjoyment!

Enjoy the fair!

5 Frederick Place,
Weymouth DT4 8HQ
///indeed.emerge.votes

"Enjoyment for all - catch it when you can!"

20

The Twisted Tree at Nothe Gardens

Summer all week, Winter Sat & Sun only
weymouthtowncouncil.co.uk

Twisting and towering up and up and up. The plump tree rests. Where all the birds nest. Hear them singing their little birdy tunes. The warm glowing sun gleams on my skin. The once sprout of a tree has emerged from the ground to grow into a lifeful beast. It sits at an angle watching over the sparkling, pristine, aqua sea. The perfect imperfections make it a unique specimen in the Nothe Fort Garden. The location in the garden is perfect to just relax and find a sense of freedom away from everyone and the disturbing noises in town. So come because this is only a taste of the sensations of the ancient tree.

Barrack Rd Nothe Fort
///noises.zealous.spine

"Perfect imperfections make it a unique specimen."

21

Newton's Cove

"Swimming all year round."

At Newton's Cove there is an abundance of swimmers, swimming all year round (but especially Autumn and Winter as it gets busy during Summer). Most of these swimmers are in a group called 'The Puddleducks', though some swim solo or are members of other groups. All seem to be wearing wetsuits and coloured bright floats in order to stay safe while swimming.

Swimming in the cold sea during the later seasons has many benefits, such as:

- Good for mental health
- Good for aches and pains

Two swimmers we talked to are named Sue and Laura who talked about how refreshing and fun it is when you swim in cold water. Some other swimmers mentioned mermaids in the water. Are they real? I guess you'll have to go to find out.

Two men at Newtons Cove, dubbed 'The Old Gits' (their words not mine) talked about the lovely views you can see from the look-out area, especially the submarines, far out in the water beyond Weymouth.

As you sit there, you can see all the huge boats going to and coming from Weymouth. During lockdown you could see six or seven large cruise ships just floating out, not far from the beach.

Look out for a tree that looks like a harp in Nothe Gardens just next to it!

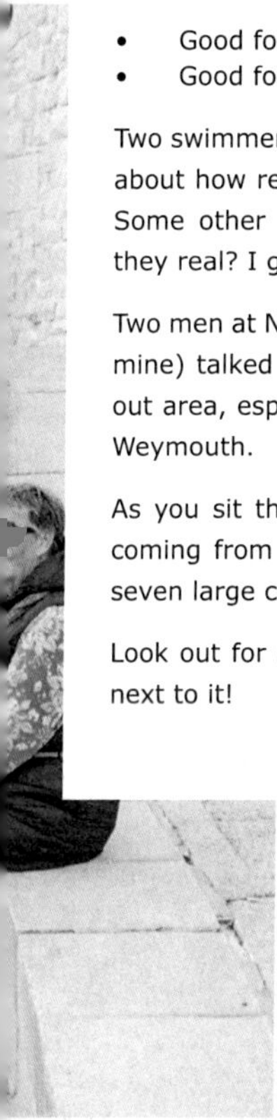

Newton's Road
DT4 8UB
/// rooms.mimic.bands

THE
FANTASTIC
GE

SAUSAGE FACTORY
HOG ROASTS

A brief (-ish) history of Weymouth

Up to the Sixteenth Century

Weymouth started as a settlement on a constricted site to the south and west of what is known as Weymouth Harbour today, in an outlying part of Wyke Regis where it developed from the 12th century onwards.

By 1252 it was established as a seaport. Melcombe Regis is considered to be the place the Black Death first got to England, about 100 years later, through a military or spice ship. Damn that paprika!

In the 1530s, Henry the Eighth built two forts on the coast to protect against an invasion from France, on whom he declared war in 1543.

* * *

17th and 18th Centuries

In 1635 100 emigrants crossed the Atlantic Ocean and landed in Massachusetts from Weymouth on a ship called Charity, deciding to name where they landed Weymouth. There are memorials to this near Weymouth Pavilion on the side of the harbour.

Shortly afterwards, during the English civil war, in February 1645, 250 people were killed in the local Crabchurch Conspiracy.

Architect Sir Christopher Wren, who designed St Paul's Cathedral, which was built of Portland's famous stone, was Weymouth's member of Parliament in 1702. He also controlled Portland's quarries from 1675 to 1717. Coincidentally Sir James Thornhill, who decorated the interior of St Paul's Cathedral, became Weymouth's MP in 1722.

The Duke of Gloucester built a large residence there named Gloucester Lodge and stayed for a winter in 1780; this resort became one of the first modern tourist destinations.

King George III made Weymouth his summer holiday residence 14 times between 1798 and 1805, even going into the sea in a bathing machine. (It was quite common back then!) A painted statue of the king is on the seafront. There is a mounted white horse representing the king carved into the chalk hills of Osmington, riding out of Weymouth rather

CONVICT
SHIP
VISITED BY ROYALTY
FINE ALES
WINES
ROYAL
OAK
INN

than towards it due to a mistake made by the creator. A myth developed that the king took offence to this due to it being a sign that the townspeople didn't welcome him.

Weymouth's esplanade is made from Georgian terraces have been converted into apartments, shops and hotels. They were constructed between 1770 and 1855, designed by architects such as James Hamilton and were commissioned by wealthy businessmen.

Along this esplanade there is the Jubilee Clock, erected to celebrate the 50th year of Queen Victoria's reign, statues of various monarchs and two war memorials.

The Royal National Lifeboat Institution first stationed a lifeboat at Weymouth on the 26th of January 1869.

There is a boathouse which was built with a slipway in the harbour and is still in use, although the lifeboat is now moored at a pontoon.

Weymouth Harbour separates Melcombe Regis and Weymouth from each other and since the 18th century has been connected with successive bridges over the narrowest part of the harbour.

The present Town Bridge, built in 1930, is a lifting bascule bridge and one of ten in the UK to let boats into the inner harbour.

The Nothe Fort, at the entrance of Weymouth Harbour and overlooking Portland, took from 1860 to 1872 to be built! Its purpose was to protect Portland's Naval Harbour. It wasn't actually used for anything other than training until World War Two where it was mainly used to deter aircraft attacks on the town. The Fort was decommissioned in 1956.

It remained unoccupied and became a victim of vandalism, falling into disrepair through lack of use. Construction to transform it into a luxury hotel was abandoned.

In 1980, The Weymouth Civic Society began to restore the Fort but was interrupted by it being used as a nuclear shelter, including the

installation of heavy blast doors, due to the Cold War.

The Nothe has since become the museum and tourist attraction that it is today, run mostly by volunteers. Its museum features original military weapons as well as static snapshots of things people in the war would have experienced. It even has interactive exhibits, for the public and local schools to gain an understanding of the history of the town.

Weymouth and Portland were bombed because of this, and a naval base on Portland during World War II.

517,816 troops embarked from the borough to fight in the Battle of Normandy.

The bouncing bomb was tested in Fleet Lagoon which is in the west of town. The history is documented at the Timewalk Museum in Brewers Quay which is a tourist attraction and shopping village.

The Punch & Judy Man

An interview with Mark Poulton

SHOW
SHOWING
TODAY

During the early stages of our project, we interviewed Mark Poulton, Weymouth's Punch and Judy man, for some more information about the entertainment that is available in the town. He started performing the Punch and Judy show in 2005 and has continued doing it in Weymouth ever since. He unfortunately couldn't perform the show during the Covid period but is looking forward to a fantastic season in 2023. We interviewed him remotely, and his backdrop was hundreds of tins of coloured paints that he uses to paint the puppets.

When did your passion for puppets start?
When I was a young boy, as soon as I watched the show at Weymouth. I knew that was what I wanted to do and I knew that my dream was to perform on Weymouth beach.

Why did you get into your career?
Insanity.

How long have you been doing the show?
Since 2005, I was 17 years old when I became interested.

How do you deal with things going wrong?
Loads of things go wrong, two weeks ago. I had the policeman puppet fall out the front of the stage.

How many puppets do you have?
Hundreds! My favourite puppet is the dog that sometimes starts the show, I had to do an inventory of each puppet for insurance.

How long is the show?
About 30 minutes but it can vary.

Where's your favourite place to do your puppet shows?
Weymouth. I always feel at home. It was always my end goal to do my show here. When I do the show, it gives me relief from reality.

Do you make your own puppets?
I make all my puppets myself, it takes about 1 month to make one if I have full concentration. I have 3 rooms in total dedicated to making puppets. I am a self taught puppet maker and my first puppet was made from driftwood I found in Wales.
I make the puppets because I have the final image in my head, and no one else can create them the way I picture each puppet.

Are you happy with where you're at in your career?
I missed summer 2022 due to a back and hip injury, as well as Covid interrupting the

performances. I missed my first performance ever due to this. During Covid, audiences averaged about 30 people and had to be distanced.

How different are the audiences?
Very, there's been a big difference over five years. Covid has meant there's a generation of children who don't know how to respond to the humour.

Do you only do your shows in Weymouth?
No, I do them in a lot of places all around the UK. I've actually met quite a few famous people when performing at places like Glastonbury and when I launched the BBC1 show. Madonna and Billie Eilish have both watched the show and I've met people like Warwick Davis and PJ Harvey at the Brits after show. I also met the Queen in 2009.

The crocodile pretends to be a cat, why?
It's a tribute to my old friend Bill, another Punch and Judy puppeteer from Aberystwyth.

What is your favourite memory of Punch & Judy show?
My first season at Weymouth was in 2005 when I first watched the show as a little boy. If I could go back to any memory in my life, I'd go back to the first time I watched the show.

Where's your favourite place to go in Weymouth?
Quiet places, I like to get away from the busyness of the beach. I like Greenhill.

Why's your job important?
To help revive Punch & Judy. People enjoy watching the show and it brings something different to Weymouth. There are only three Punch and Judy shows in the world on the beach and Weymouth is one of the three.

Is there anywhere you'd recommend to eat in Weymouth?
Cafe Blue. I first went in 2005 and was introduced to Emma, the owner. We're still friends and I've done the sign painting for them and the Curve Cafe. I also like supporting local businesses.

Do you compose the music for the show?
When I used to hear the starting music of other Punch and Judy shows when I was younger, I would drag my parents to watch. I have commissioned two people to write the music. As compared to 2005, when the licensing for fairground music was £28, as of 2019, it costs £600. By commissioning, I am no longer tied to licensing rules.

This show is
available to

*"Don't do it for the money,
do it for the passion."*

The grateful Inhabitants
To GEORGE THE THIRD
On His entering the 50th Year
Of His REIGN.
J. HAMILTON.
ARCH.T

CONCRETE POEMS

Tall dull tower
Smoke long gone
Sturdy strong bricks
Nor crumble, nor tear

Hands of kind volunteers,
Painting the yellow boat.
The careful paintbrush strokes,
Changing yellow to red.

The white modern building.
How normal it may be,
But normal can mean anything,
As two tiny men struggle to climb

Contains, parked, in all directions
Arrows: this way, that way
Clouds seeping into each other
Houses in unison towards the distance.

The calming clouds hover over the soft sand,
Making dark shadows appear.
Blue waves drag along the surface of the sand,
Bringing shiny shells to land.

Weathered, concrete, yellow boots stand
upon the harbour.
Filled to never be worn again,
Stuck, forever watching the sea
Until finally destroyed.

Wheels continuously turning
Long and blue
Snaking between rows of houses
Collecting passengers.

The tunnel, surrounded by moss,
faded into darkness
A lonely, yellow chair sitting by the entrance
An oak door on a white wall on the other side
The concrete tunnel faded into darkness.

Clouds huddling
Rustic poles supporting
The bridge as it's catered
Trampled over like it's nothing.

Red.
A good place to sit.
Tall.
Step closer, see the paintwork
is chipped.

My Town

is a hint of shapes and textures
sun glimmers off it,

steel, gold, copper,
brass full of scratches and scuffs.

It smells like a cookie box,
curry, spices, dark wood.

Feels like a place
where you just get snow

My town was loved once
but ran away, has stories to tell.

It's a good meeting place,
good for small things.

It may seem mournful,
disheartened. It's trying

to be lots of things
all at once,

It's not my Mum. I wouldn't mind
if my town went missing.

it's not a fork It's not a fork
I repeat it's not a fork

It's a clang noise,
a Viking warrior.

says 'Weymouth' over and over,
in different accents.

A collective poem

Short stories

THE 3J NIGHTMARE

By Chloe

Sarah went to Jan's when she had workers at her house. The house looks like a normal house with two floors and it's a white house and in the back garden her workers are building a pool. Jan has a boyfriend called Josh and Sarah likes him so she sets a trap for Josh.

The trap is Sarah cooks a pie and puts it on the table. He walked up to the table and sat down to eat it. Sarah came from behind and threw a blanket over him pushing him and trapped him into the room. Then she walks in and sees that it wasn't Josh - it was a builder called Jake. Sarah just stands there thinking "OMG what have I done?" and says,

"Oh hi. What's your name?"

Jake says, "My name is Jake, what's your name?"

"My name is Sarah." Sarah walks towards him slowly, Jake walks backwards as Sarah moves closer. The back door was open and when Jake was walking backwards he fell into the new swimming pool and cracked his head!

The Pavilion

by Evie

I never thought I would live to the day of me telling you this story, the story which changed my life.

I was 14, visiting Weymouth for the first time. We were going to perform a musical in the Pavilion. My very first performance. I walked into the Pavilion, my eyes darting to every corner of the theatre. It was incredible. The feeling of familiarity filled me and the warmness of the theatre consumed me. We all got ready for the musical behind the red curtains, as we could hear the theatre filling up. There must have been at least a hundred people waiting for us patiently. Suddenly we were called to stand in our places and get ready for the show to begin. I stood patiently waiting for the red curtains to lift up and for the people to be revealed. The curtains lifted suddenly and the bright lights blinded me, forcing me to close my eyes. But when I opened my eyes again, everyone had disappeared. The music had stopped and the bright light dimmed. I heard a whisper above me.

"Traitor!"

Cautiously I looked up. Bright red eyes followed my movements. Suddenly the lights became brighter revealing the hidden shadow lurking above me. I recognised him instantly, it was George Pavilion, the former owner of the Pavilion back in 1917. He jumped down onto the stage whispering "Beau traitor."

All the lights turned off, leaving only one light on, the flickering red exit sign. I ran towards it, jumping off the stage and quickly fumbling with the door handle. I opened the door, it was pitch black outside, the complete opposite to what it was like two hours ago. Everything was completely different, nothing to what it was like when I saw it earlier. The little blue house had suddenly disappeared and the whole city had been completely replaced. I saw a crumpled up newspaper rolling around on the street. I picked it up, looking at the date on it, it read 13th March 1917. The look of terror had filled my face, making my body freeze. I thought to myself

30
STOP
WALK RIGHT BACK

"How have I travelled back 100 years?"

I heard a voice behind me whispering and repeating "Traitor ... traitor."

My eyes flashed, a picture of George and I shaking hands in front of the Pavilion. A puzzled expression presented itself on my face.

"Why would I be shaking hands with George Pavilion?" I thought. It seemed as if he hated me, so why did I see the opposite? I slowly dragged my feet to the edge of the harbour, the small ripples of the water was all I could hear. The voices were gone and the whispering had stopped. His voice replayed in my head and it felt familiar. I glanced back at the Pavilion. How did a place I had never seen before feel like.... home? Creeping slowly back to the Pavilion, quiet little whispers appeared from the darkness, making me shiver. I entered the theatre for a second time, but this time, every seat was full and what looked like an older version of me was on the stage. I leant on the back wall, observing everything that was happening. Confusion consumed me. "What was even happening?" I thought to myself and tapped on George Pavilion's shoulder. He didn't turn around, nor did he flinch. It felt as if I was invisible. I stood in front of what looked like me, but somehow I didn't appear to be blocking her vision. Cautiously I got off the stage and sat on the floor to observe what was unfolding. Suddenly a loud voice boomed.

"Now I present to you the new owner of the Pavilion Theatre!" A bright light shone, blinding me once more. Somehow I was on the stage, being handed the keys to the Pavilion.

George quietly muttered under his breath "Traitor" as I held the keys in my hands. He looked back at the audience, cheerfully smiling, trying to hide his bittersweet expression. The flash of a camera forced me to close my eyes. It seemed as if I was no longer invisible; all of the audience's focus was on me. I walked off the stage, people congratulating me all around. The photographer handed me the photo he just took. I quietly gasped as I saw myself in the picture. I looked completely different. It seemed as if I was no longer fourteen, but I was actually around the age of thirty. My body froze. How could I tell if this was real life or not? Is this all real? I ran backstage and shortly screamed as I looked in the mirror. It was real. Everything that I saw was true. Somehow I wasn't fourteen, I wasn't a little girl, I was in a completely different year and I was twice my age.

SHORT STORY LONG

By Kayden

One day in an old house, there was a ghost of some kind. A figment of your imagination, he had lived in that house for over a century. Nobody had ever lived there because of how old it was, but this was about to change.

My family and I were driving to the house in pouring rain and hurricane-like winds.

The ghost had noticed us, specifically me. As we got closer every step caused harder and harder winds, finally we made it inside the house.

As I stepped into the house with my mum and dad, they told me to go upstairs and choose a room, of course I chose the biggest room. I could see movement in the corner of the room, I ignored it at first but then I decided to take a look. I went and I saw a strange floating creature, I was both interested and scared, all of a sudden it began to talk.

"Hello" said the creature.

I replied saying "Hello, what are you?" There was no response then in a flash, it was gone!

My parents ran up saying "Are you ok?, who were you talking to?"

Me being only six I just stared and said....

STEAMPUNK BIRD

By Carwyn

It was a dark rainy night in Weymouth, the streets were barren except a single streetlight and a lonely man who walked down the dark streets. He did so every night in the hope he would find someone, to be lonely no more. The man was invisible to most, nobody wanted to talk to him not even the most desperate of souls; beggars and salesmen refused to beg for his help and shopkeepers would take a while to notice him. The man was lonely and that was that.

He got to the streetlight to have a rest when he saw something strange. A man cloaked in shadows, only one eye visible, walked up to him.

He carried an aura that was reassuring, as if he were an old friend.

"Why, hello there!"

The man stared in shock, he was actually noticed.

"Say, you look quite lonely,"

The man nodded sadly.

"Well I have just the thing you need." The stranger held his hand out.

"Avian Punk." The stranger held out his hand seemingly for a handshake.

The streetlight malfunctioned flickering rapidly until it went completely off. When the light returned the stranger was no longer there, only a small box with a strange picture of a bird on it.

The man picked up the box and continued on his way home. After a long walk he sat on his cold, black sofa contemplating whether he should open the box, until a wave of curiosity swept over him and he gave in to his desire. Inside the box was a small statue of a bird seemingly made of Steampunk technology surrounded by salt.

He took the bird from the box. It felt familiar, but when he did it started to expand, growing to the size of his sofa, developing limbs.

The man sprinted to his door, unlocking it while the bird chased him. It pursued him outside of the house, chasing while only growing bigger with larger and more joints, until they reached the streetlight.

The man was out of breath, the bird looked down upon him, it was now 15 feet tall, when it suddenly lunged at him skewering him with its beak, destroying the man's whole body.

When he awoke he was stuck in a dark cold ball. It smelled like dried blood and metal? He banged on the walls of the ball as the metal thumping echoed in the ball, suddenly drowned out by a screeching.

The bird sat awaiting the stranger. When he came, as fast as he'd left, he picked up the bird and whispered ... "Now you'll never be alone again."

Lavender

By Elle

As Marie closed the large wooden door behind Jonathon, sunlight filling her house, she squealed with excitement at the thought of spending the rest of her life with her one love. She thought of everything she could do before he returned and immediately set out to do them. On the first day Marie baked cookies for all her neighbours. When they had finished in the oven Marie wrapped them all in coloured bows; giddy with excitement at the thought of one day baking for children of her own. She carefully placed each cookie into her delicately weaved basket and left her home, leaving the thick smell of sweetness behind her.

Day 2: Picked some of her favourite flowers- flower arranging, crowns etc.

Day 3: Clean the house- scrubbing floors, changing sheets.

Day 4: Cooked a grand dinner for Jonathon's arrival.

Day 5: Waiting- hears about the village Jonathon was in- disaster (killings?)

Day 6: Waiting

Day 7: As Marie stared at the dull wooden door, she wondered if her nightmares had come true. She didn't dare move her eyes off the door, at the forever slimming chance that her love would return to her. Hours passed and Marie began to feel heavy tears smother her face. She stood on her shaky frail legs and slowly walked towards her and Jonathon's bedroom, passing the withering food that had been prepared for Jonathon. Shaking, Marie opened her bedroom door and made her way over to the arsenic she kept in her drawer. She picked it up with her thin bony fingers and placed it into her mouth. Just as Marie felt herself slipping out of consciousness she heard the front door open and the sweet small of lavender filled her senses.

Ghastly Luck

By Dalia

The sun is slowly setting, showing off all the blooming colours filling the sky as the haunted night comes alive. Everyone's had a scrumptious dinner and all are ready to watch their favourite family show. But unlucky for Tom he needed his glasses and being the strong boy he is, nothing really bothered him, he started climbing up the stairs in the dark. But to his surprise something was standing in front of him, something humanlike, but that was impossible, everyone was downstairs. He froze to focus his eyes, get used to the pitch black surroundings, and see what the figure was.

Then he realised it was this youthful lady glaring straight at him. She had elegant slick long dark hair and smooth pale skin that almost blended in with her old fashioned night gown. She was just positioned lifeless on one of the stairs, leaning over a bit just observing, not speaking, no noise just the piercing eyes staring in his soul. He was stuck! He felt trapped and lost. His feet wouldn't proceed forward nor back. The atmosphere of this girl completely paralyzed his whole body. An apparition. Fortunately for him the call from his parent broke the hypnosis.

"Honey her show is about to start."

"Coming!" he replied.

Running down, having no thoughts about his glasses, but as he made the last stair he slowly rotated his neck to check on the ghost but only to witness the figure was gone! The feeling of annoyance came to him as he still needed his glasses! Entering the living room, feeling stumped, he noticed the 'favourite' family TV show was the one that he was dreading to watch: the boring Riverdale.

MOONLIT

By Jaimey

Releasing, twirling, crunching: the aging auburn leaves gather at Faun's feet. Gravel grinding as she ponders further, meeting with the forest. Faun finds herself a turned over log and rests upon it. Pulling out her notepad and pen she scribbles to check the ink works. A hush hollows throughout the forest and the only noise is the stream water trickling past her ankles and the calling of the desperate mother bird awaiting her children. Scratching and scurrying are the titian squirrels searching for their winter stash suffocated by its overgrown branches. The forest resembled a sprawling fortress, barricading the creatures from the dangers of the outside world. A few last minute touches are made to

Faun's art piece then she gathers her things and rises up from the log. Just as she was about to walk, a soft humming sound came from down the river. Intrigued, she followed the trail, meeting with the lake, so beautiful and demure.

A plethora of stars are painted along the luminous sky, the canvas overhead reflects the moonlit body of water. If one was to look too close they would see a peculiar glowing blue light submerged underneath the surface. The air was bitter but filled with optimism. The song continued onwards getting louder with every step Faun took.

Suddenly out from the depths of the lake rose a magnificent slimy species. At first glance it was clear to see this was no human. Turquoise scales crawled from below the waist revealing a fascinating tail with fins at the tip. Although she was not human she did have a human face. Dainty freckles splattered across her fair skin and diminutive waterdrops hung from her perfect lips. She called out to Faun with so much beauty it was hypnotising. She used her harmonic voice to beckon Faun towards her. Now inches apart, the peculiar being reached out her ocean kissed hand and placed her bleak fingertips onto Faun's shoulder. She could smell her cinnamon breath against her cheek.

The trees surrounding them assembled strategically like a battalion of soldiers peering across the velvet landscape. Before anything else could occur, the odour of thick, black smoke choked out from the forest's lungs. It was now obvious as the fierce flames roared, as they scratched up the trees, swallowing all the life and spitting it back out again.

Where's Sam?

By Tyler

A normal day, yet a quiet one.

No customers.

Sam, a friendly bartender working for minimum wage, grieving his mother's death. He tries to move on and gets out the cleaning equipment. While cleaning he hears a strange noise from the dark, gloomy hallway.

When turning the lights on a strange familiar place is reminded, some might call it a limital space, deja-vu. The dark red carpets and the beige wall give me an unsettling feeling. The strangely attractive noise comes from room 13.

He enters and never exits.

The manager wonders where he is.

"Sam! Where are you? We need to open up!"

No reply from upstairs. "Sam!"

She walks upstairs and looks in every room, even room 13, they were all empty.

People say that they see two spirits, hiding from all life, one dressed like a bartender, one with long hair in all white robes.

Food! Food! Food!

By Freya

A chip flies in and lands beneath me.

"This is my chance!" I scream to myself.

My eyes dart left to right and back again, no chance to hang around. I launch my whole body towards it. I can feel the harsh breeze against my wing, deep desperation to secure the prize.

Before I know it, I've hit the scorching floor. I lower my beak and completely inhale it. I fly up on top of my roof and take a perch, the bright colour bombards my mind. I peer over to see the sea shimmering in the sunlight and the familiar smoke fills my nostrils. And yet again, the cycle begins, continues and never stops.

As the sun descends I hear the chirps travelling around me. I find comfort in this, just knowing that I am not alone.

CEC

By Lily

Cecelia or Cec, as they were nicknamed by Lily, was nearing Weymouth and the dreary weather was not what they expected of the small seaside town. It was very different from the sunny Holland they'd flown from and called home. They hadn't slept much on the long, dull bus drive down from the airport, other than the occasional doze that was swiftly interrupted by their rowdy class mates, though the incessant noise that chorused through the bus wasn't the only thing keeping them up. They had a thought, a hope, at the back of their mind that they might bump into their friend, Lily, during their visit to England. Little did they know their close friend actually lived in Weymouth.

They let the thought leave their mind and went back to listening to Katy

Perry and doodling their character Kizzie in their notebook. Cec briefly glanced out the window and something peculiar caught their eye. A girl with long white hair and dirty yet elegant attire staring at them.... smiling....

Soon they arrived at their destination and many of Cec's classmates began piling out of the large blue and white bus that had held them hostage for the past three hours. Their first impression of Weymouth was not the best; as it was quite late when they arrived and rain was pouring all around them. The darkness and the poor weather caused the usually cheery town to appear very creepy. Their teachers herded the class onto the pavement and after doing the register Cec felt an excited tap on their shoulder. They cautiously turned around, but their worrying subsided when they saw a familiar freckled face.

"Lili!" they exclaimed, very happy there was someone they knew in a town full of strangers.

"Cec!" Lily shouted slightly too loudly, the brunette pulled the blonde into a tight hug.

"I'm so happy you're here!"

The two friends chatted for a while before Cec's teacher called them over.

Lily noticed a strange looking girl in the group of tired students. A girl with bright white hair and a very long glamorous gown. She seemed to be looking at Cec. The look in the girl's eyes made Lily shudder with horror.....

Destined to be alone

By Blair

"I'll love you forever," Delilah whispered to her lover as they danced in the massive ballroom. Delilah then began to explore and stumbled upon a dimly lighted room with no windows. As she walked in, the door slammed behind her with an aggressive force. She began to panic manically, looking around the room as raindrops were smashing against the roof. She found a switch and as soon as she turned it on she was met with a massive bouquet of flowers with a note with her name on it. Her face flushed with fear as there was no way in and why would she write a letter to herself?

The letter read

Dear Delilah,

I love you, I have always loved you and I know you don't feel the same way, but soon you will see how deep my love for you is.

Sincerely, Louis

Click! She heard the door open and quickly ran out desperately running to the ballroom, a million thoughts running through her head "What's going on? Where's Anna? What's Louis doing?"

She burst into the ballroom expecting the worst, but...

Everything was normal, everyone was still dancing, she looked over the room in confusion, wondering what Louis had actually done. Delilah continued to scan the room aggressively, searching for her lover. She froze as she saw her girlfriend Anna sat in the corner quietly sobbing into her hands. Delilah ran over to comfort her, but quickly realised she couldn't.

She was dead.

The Demonic Baker

By Dominick

The cook always seems to be working, all day, every day with no stops, but he always makes the best bread, pastries and cakes. Nobody can resist the smell of fresh food when walking outside the bakery. However, anybody who sees the recipe is never seen again.

Jessica Blueman was walking to her college one day when she decided to take a shortcut through the street the bakery was on. Little did she know that this would be the worst mistake of her life. Somehow, the world shifted, everything seemed different. Wrong even. The cracks in the road expanded and bellowing winds shook the trees. Jessica ran as fast as she could when she caught the marvellous smell of freshly baked pastries. Everything calmed. Nothing was wrong anymore. Everything was perfect; birds were singing, there were no clouds in the sky and most importantly : the luscious smell of baking. It was irresistible, she had to go in. How could she not?

When she pushed the crystal blue door the nostalgic sound of a bell rang in her ears. More dopamine rushed to her brain. The chequered chess-like floor satisfied her senses. She made her move towards the counter. She looked around the building. Retro style walls were perfection. She felt as if she was in a fever dream. Nothing could stop her now, she was going to buy something in the bakery, anything...

As she edged closer to the baker, nausea filled her brain again. Sweet scented smoke filled her nose. With her final remaining steps she grabbed the baker's beige polyester blazer. Tortuous pain that shattered her ears replaced the dizziness. The cook's head snapped 180° to face her with a deathly stare. His glowing pearl white eyes cracked his own glasses and blinded Jessica like looking at a thousand suns. Soon she could not feel anything. Senses gone. Memories gone. All taken from her. Stolen from her. The only thing that remained was rage. Chaotic rage. The need for revenge.

When she opened her dry, blistering eyes she was different. The baker's eyes faded back to normal as she felt her soul floating away. Jessica whimpered, "No he can't do this, please don't do this." She lunged from her squirming position on the floor and ripped out his ghostly eye from his wrinkled, melting face. The baker let out a demonic scream, he staggered back for a second before punching her with inhuman speed. His severed eye flung onto the off-white wall. The eye smashed to dust, like glass shattering. It seemed as if a tornado had just started as lightning fast winds circled inside the bakery. All the tools lifted up and flew directly at the baker, as if they had been thrown, they impaled him throughout his body like bullets. The baker fell to the floor as if he was in slow motion. Suddenly Jessica felt alive again. She could remember again. As she blinked she appeared outside of the bakery. However when she looked back it had disappeared. Replaced by the same generic building beside it.....

The Creature I saw that night

By Christabelle

It was a still calm night and I decided to go for a swim in the cove. I walked along the esplanade and it was quiet since no one was around. The sun began to set and the sky started to turn dark. The sunset was beautiful that night. I was approaching the cove and I put my bag down. I looked out at the water and I noticed the water was partially clear tonight. In the distance there was a murky patch of water and I thought I saw a small splash.

I know I saw something because there was a ripple in the water in the spot I saw the splash. There! Another splash! This time I know that I was not imagining it. I turned to get my binoculars out of my bag and out of the corner of my eye I see it... a tentacle. I start to panic. I am by myself and I have no signal on my phone. I'm scared, but intrigued.

The creature was about ten metres away but it was slowly approaching closer. The closer it comes, the more of it I see. I'm sure that I can see about eight tentacles. I stand for about five minutes and just stare at the water and the creature and the water and the creature again. Without warning the creature disappears and just like that the water was clear again.

This is odd. This sounds like something out of a newspaper that you'd read about, or watch in a movie say that isn't real. I decided that since the water was so clear and so calm that I'd go for a swim. After all, whatever I'd seen had gone. I decided to go in. Cautiously I placed my foot into the water. It was calm and quiet. Very quiet. Too quiet.....

I looked up at the sky, the sky was a midnight shade of black, as black as coal. I gazed at the bright full moon and the thousands of beautiful twinkling stars. All so bright. I could make out a few of the constellations: Aquarius, Aries. There's Venus, the brightest star in the sky! I could stand there all evening, mesmerised by the wonders of that night sky.

All of a sudden "Ouch!" I could feel something on my leg, probably seaweed I thought, or a fish swimming past. OUCH! There it is again but this time it hurt more, it felt like someone, something was gripping me, the grip tightening rapidly by the second.. I looked down.

"This is it, " I said, "this is how I die".......

Imagined WORLDS

Imagined WORLDS

Imagined WORLDS

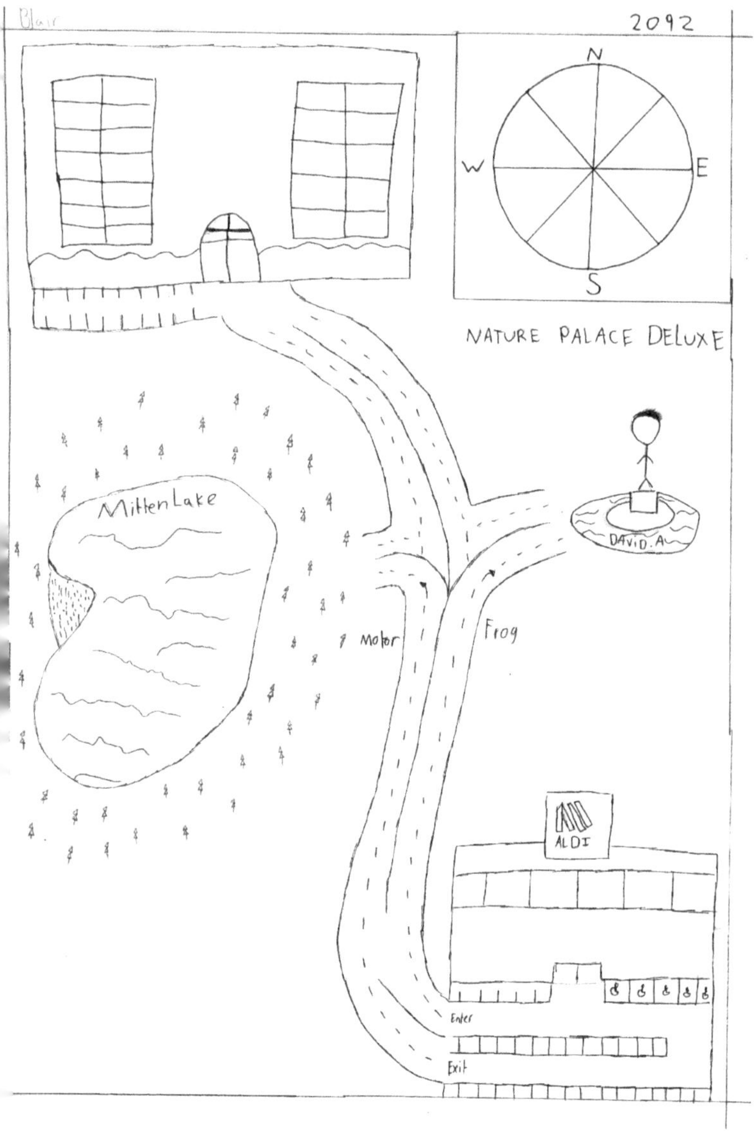
Blair
2092
N
W
E
S
NATURE PALACE DELUXE
MittenLake
DAVID.A
Motor
Frog
ALDI
Enter
Exit

Greeni 2023
THE ONE PIECE IS REAL
Peri Peri

Minnesota
???
N
NW
NE
W
E
SW
SE
S
GoAL

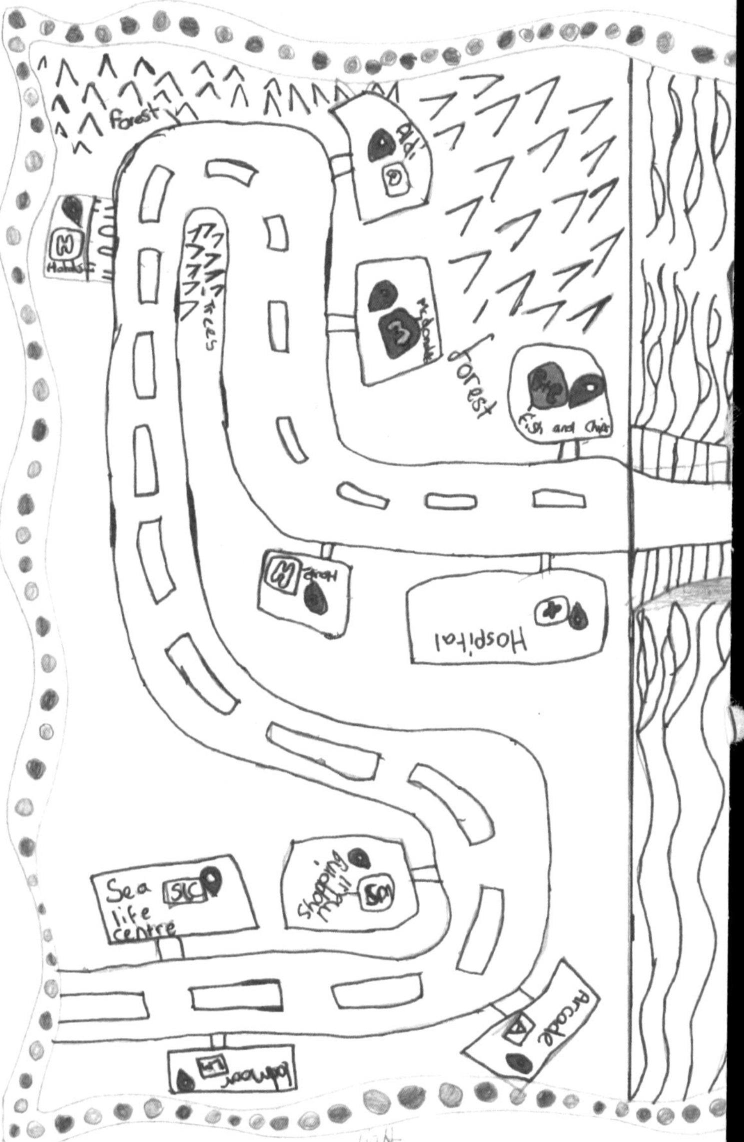
Forest
Aldi
Trees
Forest
Fish and Chips
Hospital
Sea life centre
SLC
Shopping Mall
SM
Arcade

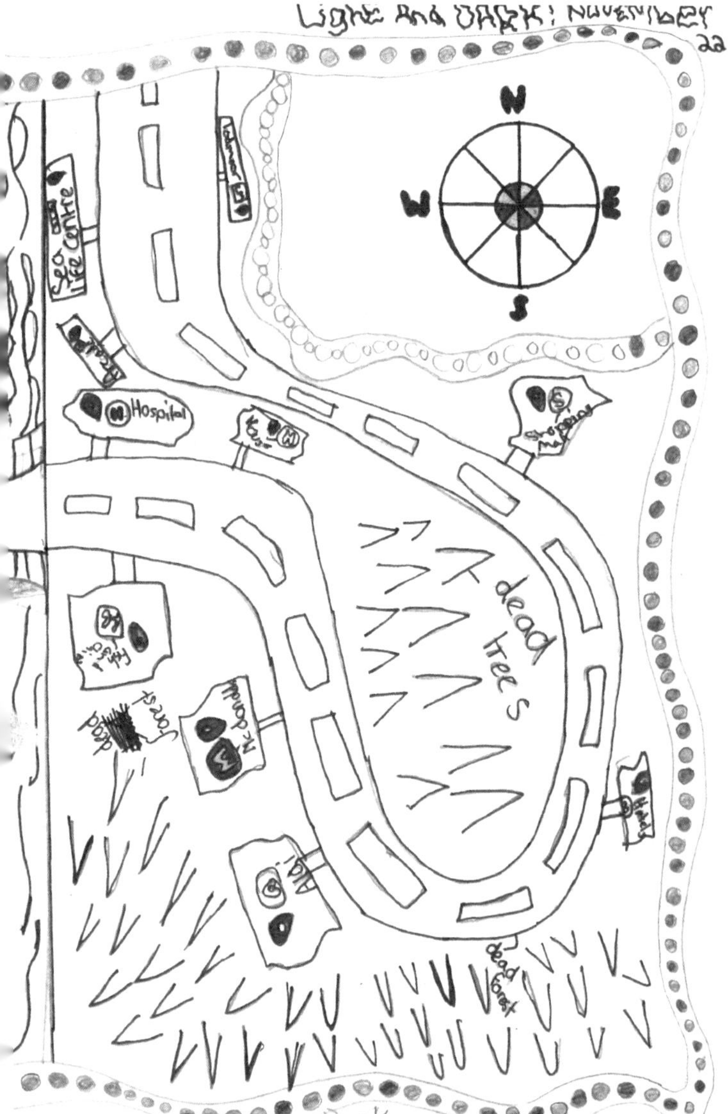
Light And DARK: November 22
N
S
E
W
Sea life Centre
Hospital
dead trees
Mc Donalds
forest
dead forest
Dark

ZOO
Nutrition Bar!
All your
yum!
Golden Supply Crate
Hover train
fun land
26 febuary
2023
by Bob
INFINIT
WATER

Taylor Swift • Fearless • Speak now • Red • 1989 • Reputation • Lover •
folklore • Evermore • Midnights • (Taylor's version) • Born to die • Paradise • Ultra violence • Honeymoon •
e banisters • Chemtrails over the country club • Norman F*** Rockwell! • Lust for life
Old Money Island · 2037 · By Jaimey
Key:
- Live music
- Coffee shop
- Library
- Forest
- Country club
N
E
S
W
•Cola Strt
•Radio Road
Brooklyn•
Mariners Apartment complex
•Ultraviolet Nightclub
•Autumn
•Spring
•Winter
Folklore Forest
•Summer
Chemtrails
Country club
•Lolita Lane
Carmen Cafe•
West Coast
•Vintage tea
•Snow at the beach

CITY OF LIGHT
(3023)
N
E

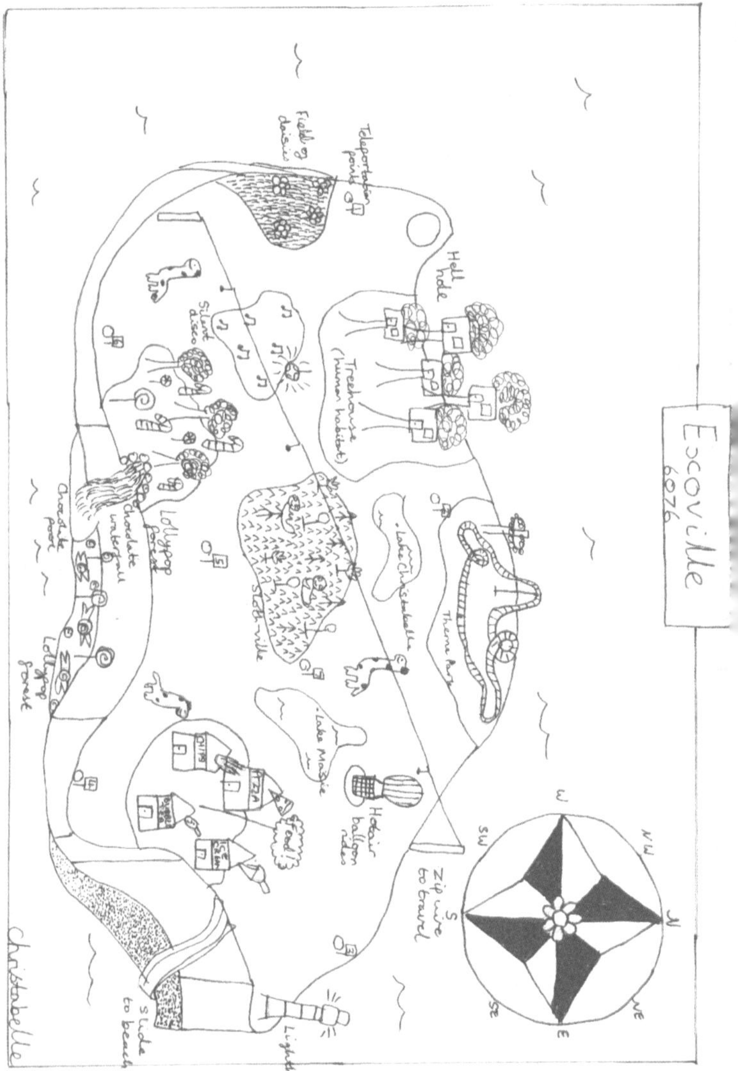
Escoville
6076
Teleportation point
Field of daisies
Hell hole
Silent disco
Treehouse (human habitat)
Lollypop forest
Chocolate waterfall
Chocolate pool
Sloth-ville
Lake Christabelle
Theme park
Hot air balloon rides
Zip wire to travel
Lighthouse
Slide to beach
Christabelle
N
NE
E
SE
S
SW
W
NW

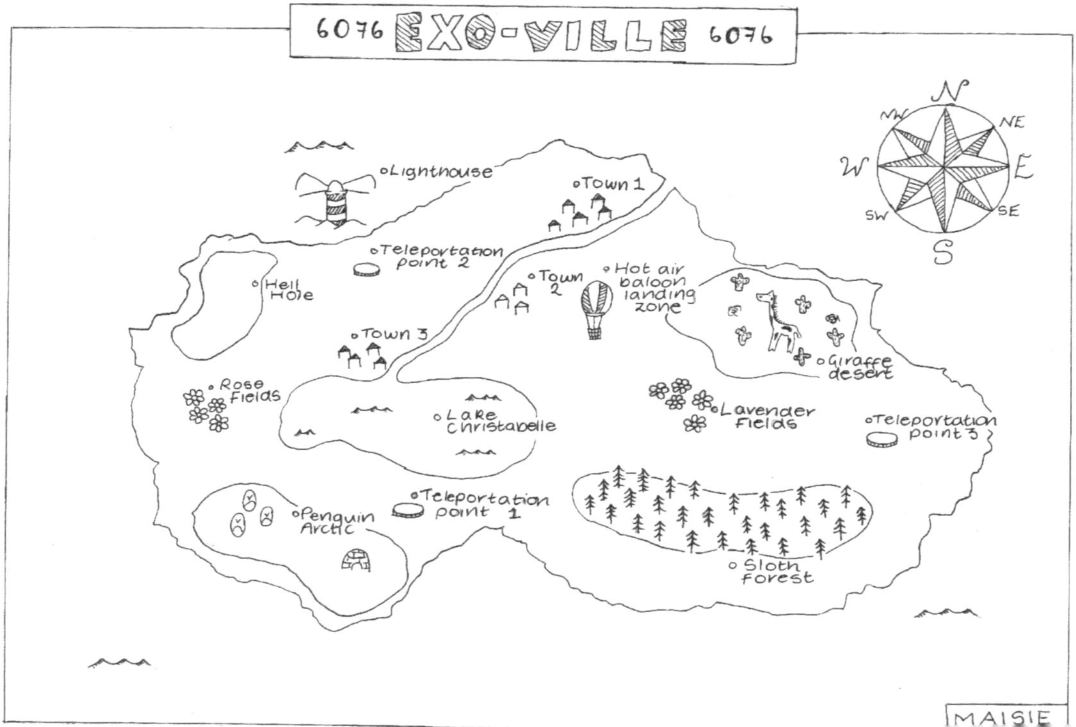
6076 EXO-VILLE 6076
Lighthouse
Town 1
Teleportation point 2
Hell Hole
Town 2
Hot air baloon landing zone
Town 3
Rose Fields
Lake Christabelle
Giraffe desert
Lavender Fields
Teleportation point 3
Teleportation point 1
Penguin Arctic
Sloth forest
N
NE
E
SE
S
SW
W
NW
MAISIE

•MUSIC ZONE•
Sports
Acadamy
•SHOPS•

N
W
E
S
·ANIMAL LAND·
→A MAP OF←
WEYMOUTH
FOOTBALL EDITION
23-11-2022

The Project

The brief for this project was to work with a mixed cohort of Year 9's from Budmouth Academy to create and produce an alternative guide to Weymouth, the key ingredient being creativity and creative thinking.

At the start of the first workshop they filed in huffing, puffing and panting and bemoaning the sixty stair climb, somewhat bemused by the project and having time out from their usual lessons.

I asked "What is Weymouth?" Responses included 'A town, a home, my town, a place, a holiday destination, a seaside resort.'

An independent creative writing task entitled, 'There's nothing better about Weymouth than...' brought more depth to what Weymouth meant to them and we took it from there.

We went on a tour around the town. Sea swimmers were interviewed, bubble tea was sampled, Polaroids taken and the final destination, the library, was enjoyed by all. Walking, talking, experiencing, observing and thought sharing fired up their enthusiasm and brought everyone closer together as a group.

Using a large bedsheet we created a map, stapling the Polaroids into position and drawing the outline of the route taken. It was draped over the classroom whiteboard and became the centrepiece for the workshops. Throughout the weeks we entertained a variety of guests, including a ghost story writer, a map maker, a poet, the long established Punch and Judy entertainer and a homeless pigeon (don't ask). To question and challenge the value of the project, the 'Bank Manager' rang at various intervals on a large old fashioned phone placed in the centre of the workshop. This added a different dimension to the project and kept the students entertained and motivated, with the surety of the outcome giving them a sense of purpose. Throughout the ten weeks we embraced a wealth of experiences; mindful tasting of jelly babies, creating poetry around a model railway track, detailed observations of spoons twisting into poetry. The students embraced every challenge, absorbed each task and consistently gave 100%.

They were playful in their approach and fantastic to work with and this guide is the fruit of their labours. I've observed their confidence grow, I've listened in on their conversations, overheard snippets that revealed so much about their Weymouth and what it means to them. Just another seaside town… no way! I have been educated.

I have been overwhelmed by the generosity of the volunteers, their creative input, observations and feedback, the sensitive support they gave the students and their input into the project as a whole has been invaluable.

And then came the completed evaluations. In one of the boxes on a form entitled SOMETHING I HAVE LEARNT, a student wrote "Imagination is endless (so use it)."

My job was done!

Rowan Beecham
Workshop Leader

Notes

About The Bank of Dreams & Nightmares

OUR MISSION STATEMENT

Everyone's full of stories. Don't believe me? Well then, off to bed and see for yourself. For when you sleep the stories in your head wake up. Your dreams and nightmares come alive and start to play in a world of infinite possibility and never-ending imagination. And then you wake up. And reality brings them crashing to an end, cruelly concluding all that could have been. Well we're here to put an end to that, or at least a beginning. 1000s and 1000s of beginnings. Hear ye hear ye! We at the Bank of Dreams & Nightmares want your stories. Bring them in, in all their absurd, weird and wonderful starts, middles or ends. And we'll keep your story alive, keep it going, bringing it out of your head and into the cold but illuminating light of day. And we won't stop there. Oh no. Every story deposited in the Bank of Dreams & Nightmares gets interest. Like any good bank we'll help your investment grow and grow. We'll give it eyes and ears to see and hear it, words to appreciate it, and applause to motivate it on. So believe in what's in your head, believe in what you can create, believe in your dreams and nightmares.

Our aim

get more kids writing and show them just how far their words can take them.

by

making them realise their weird, wonderful, absurd, ridiculous ideas are all story-worthy

promising

that if they deposit them in our bank we'll bring them to life and help them accrue interest (i.e. eyes and ears to see and hear them)

THE INSPIRATION

826 Valencia in San Francisco

WHAT WE DO

We are a registered charity offering FREE creative writing workshops to children aged 7-18 in the West Dorset area of the UK. We want to show children just how far their words and stories can take them, so we work with industry professionals to create inspirational workshops that all have a real world outcome. How about writing a campaign for a cause you feel strongly about and then seeing it made by professionals so you can present it to local government or businesses? What if you wrote some song lyrics, and are then able to see a real musical artist take your words and make it into a real recording you can share with the world? Or how about you become the lead defence lawyer for a special mock trial in a real court house where your persuasive arguments determine whether someone is guilty or not guilty? The possibilities are endless, and at The Bank of Dreams & Nightmares we want to have fun showing children that it all starts with an idea, a story, some words and where that can take you is the exciting part.

Our focus is on those children who are most under-resourced, who normally do not have access to these types of things but deserve them just as much as anyone else.

One day we hope to be housed in a real bank in Bridport, although instead of money we deal in the currency of stories.

We offer after school clubs for children to develop their writing and get involved in longer workshop projects that currently range from creating their own quarterly newspaper to a sketch comedy workshop, with the final sketches being made by professional actors.

The Bank of Dreams & Nightmares is committed to practically addressing educational inequalities and the opportunity gap faced by young people from less advantaged backgrounds. We work in communities with high levels of socio-economic inequality, where we are providing a critical link between local schools, arts organisations, higher education institutions, and the commercial sector.

Our aim is to help children and young people to discover and harness the power of their own imaginations and creative writing skills. The Bank of Dreams & Nightmares strives to improve children's behaviour, engagement, essential life skills and wellbeing - the root causes of exclusion.

At its core The Bank of Dreams & Nightmares is also about something much broader and more inclusive: it is about using the creative practice of writing and storytelling to help local children and teenagers from all backgrounds to be resilient, creative, and successful shapers of their own lives.

IMPACT

Through our programmes, young writers feel listened to and have their opinions valued and acted upon. We can demonstrate the impact creative writing has on young people. We provoke and empower them to think creatively and help them unlock their imaginations. Then we publish their writing, providing purpose and value. The impact is shown through significant shifts in motivation, attitude, and behaviours - which in turn affects health, ambition and resilience.

OUR WORKSHOPS

Primary School
Storymaking workshop

In this two and a half hour workshop we work with a class to collectively create a story, whilst one of our volunteer illustrators brings the story to life as it happens. The first half of the session has the class of young writers voting and creating as a group, as one of our volunteers scribes the story for them. Once they get to the cliffhanger moment each writer then creates their own ending to the story, with the help of our story mentors. After the session we take the words and pictures and make them into a beautiful bound book with each participant getting their own author biog at the back and space to create their individual ending. It is always a fun and lively session and the results have been wonderful.

Secondary School
Podcasting workshop

In this one-off workshop we work with a class of young writers to develop a personal essay. The workshop normally lasts around four hours as we explore different aspects of the self and what it means to our writers. It is always a lively and interactive session and the final outcome is to record each essay as a podcast, which is broadcast via our soundcloud page.

Secondary School
10 Week Story Anthology

In this longer programme we work with groups of students to develop an anthology or guide book based on a chosen theme. We work closely with the school to decide on a theme which complements the curriculum for the chosen year group. At the end of the six weeks we make the final anthology into a published book, one of which you are reading now. All the proceeds from the sales of the book go directly back into the charity.

The Vault Newspaper

This is our after school workshop that takes place every Thursday during term time. Here we work with a group of young writers between 10 and 15 years of age to create a quarterly subscription-based newspaper. In the issue we look back at the news from the last three months and the writers share their perspectives on the news stories that they have selected.

PEOPLE

Founder:
Nick Goldsmith
Creative learning manager:
Ed Swift
Volunteer Coordinator:
Alex Green
Board of Directors:
Mick Smith, Simon Deverell, Joel Collins,
Niki McCretton, Simon Hawkins, Jess Morency

OUR VOLUNTEERS

There is absolutely no way any of this would be possible without our incredible volunteers. These incredible people work in all realms, from story mentoring to illustrating and beyond. They range in age, background and expertise but all have a shared passion for our work with young people. We salute you!

IT'S ALWAYS A GOOD TIME TO GIVE!

We need your help

We are always seeking new volunteers to help out either as story mentors, illustrators, or simply as experts in their fields. It is very simple to join as a volunteer, and we try and make it a lot of fun in the process. You do not need to be a writer or have an educational background, you just need to be able to listen and encourage our young writers to express themselves.

Please fill out our online application to let us know how you may be able to help, and to come along to one of our training sessions. Tea and cake provided!

More information at thebankofdreamsandnightmares.org/volunteering

Other ways to give

Whether it's loose change or heaps of cash, a donation of any size will help us continue to offer a variety of FREE writing workshops to children in the West Dorset area.

Please make a donation at: thebankofdreamsandnightmares.org/donate

Or email us at **nick@thebankofdreamsandnightmares.org** to discuss how you may be able to help.

All proceeds from the sale of this book go toward funding free student programming at The Bank of Dreams & Nightmares.

"Don't Feed The Locals"
has been made possible with the generous help of ...

Jurassic Fibre

"It's been a real pleasure for Jurassic Fibre to support the Bank of Dreams and Nightmares, seeing what these young creative thinkers can produce. Those with keen eyes will spot the Jurassic Fibre engineer up a pole next to our van on the map! Rolling out our ultrafast full fibre broadband network across Weymouth and Dorset will give more children access to resources that enable their creativity, upskill them and ensure they're fully a part of their local community."

Annabel McCabe
Events & Sponsorship Manager with Jurassic Fibre

Other books available from the vaults at The Bank of Dreams & Nightmares:

Available at Little Toller Books in Beaminster and The Book Shop in Bridport plus online via our website. All proceeds go directly into funding more workshops run by the charity.

Subscribe to our quarterly newspaper

What's going on?

created entirely by children attending our workshop.

www.thebankofdreamsandnightmares.org